William Bausman

The Protégé

SALZWASSER
VERLAG

William Bausman

The Protégé

Reprint of the original, first published in 1859.

1st Edition 2022 | ISBN: 978-3-37513-350-4

Verlag (Publisher): Salzwasser Verlag GmbH, Zeilweg 44, 60439 Frankfurt, Deutschland
Vertretungsberechtigt (Authorized to represent): E. Roepke, Zeilweg 44, 60439 Frankfurt, Deutschland
Druck (Print): Books on Demand GmbH, In de Tarpen 42, 22848 Norderstedt, Deutschland

THE PROTÉGÉ,

A POEM,

BY WILLIAM BAUSMAN.

DELIVERED

At the Metropolitan Theater on the 26th of April 1859, being the occasion
of the Fortieth Anniversary of the Introduction of Odd Fellowship
into the United States, commemorated by the United
Lodges and Encampment of the
Sacramento Division.

SACRAMENTO:
PUBLISHED BY JOHN J. MURPHY, BOOKSELLER,
Corner of J and Fourth Streets.

1859.

INTRODUCTION.

THE dramatist, whose story lacks a hero
Bloody and terrible, goes back to Nero,
Or Tarquin, or Caligula, or Draco—
    Names to a tragedy rather ornamental—
When bowie-knives, revolvers and tobacco
    Were little known or used; and sentimental
Episodes among the ladies, transpired
After a fashion truly to be admired.
Roman Lucretia covered her disgrace
    By self-destruction. She was a heroine;
The proudest and the loveliest of her race,
    And very different in her style from mine.
Her's was a noble geneaology,
Plucking its trophies from a family tree;
Mine is bogus, tinseled, and presuming;

INTRODUCTION.

Deficient in the power of illuming
A wholesome moral, acted on the stage,
Or rounded period to a written page.

The muse says thus much in extenuation
   To her defects of incident and plot;
Hoping to win the reader's approbation
    Whether her effort merits it or not.
The poem aims to satirize frivolity
In certain people, of a spurious quality,
And is at least indiginous, however
It fails in object, or detailed endeavor.

DEDICATORY ODE.

When the Cycles first begun,
Marked by courses of the sun,
Time and Space, of instant birth,
Occupied and ruled the earth;
Then the destinies of man
Were interwoven with the plan.
Tyrants flourished, kings arose;
Nations armed themselves as foes;
Freedom shrieked and wept in vain,
O'er her heroes crushed and slain;
Still the crimson tide flowed on,
Whether foe or ally won;
Still the desecrating flood
Flows in streams of human blood.

Is there no arresting hand
Stretching out o'er all the land?
No Samaritan abroad,
Clothed with attributes from God?
No elixir, sweet and pure,
Malady like this to cure?
No encircling chain to bind,
One in heart and one in mind,

Every nation, every tongue
From a common parent sprung?

"Yes!" an angel voice exclaims:
"Here behold the golden.chains;
Numbering exactly three—
Emblems of Fraternity!
One for FRIENDSHIP; such as truth
Kindles in the heart of youth;
One for LOVE; so closely knit,
That passion may not sever it.
One for TRUTH, which binds the whole
With a single thought and soul:
Three in one, and one in three—
A unit and a trinity!"

Bondsmen we, of boastful hight,
Mingling in a secret right;
Fettered with a mystic tie;
Watched by the All-Seeing Eye;
Interchanging social thought,
By true fellowship begot.
All our aims, and all our ends,
Whether to our foes or friends,
Are to elevate the mind,
War on vice of every kind;
Soothe the pillow of distress,
Educate the fatherless;
Win a title-deed to be
WORTHY this Fraternity.

PART I.

IN ALL the city, gay beyond comparison,
None outshone the charming Mrs. Harrison ;
Two husbands buried, with the wealth of each,
She claimed a rank above the vulgar reach.
Her origin—why should we pause to trace it ?
Two wedded names were ample to deface it.
Her maiden troth was plighted at a season
 When fluttering pulses warm each youthful
  vein,
And passion prompts beyond the power of reason
 Its headlong course to govern or restrain.

A

That morrow came, when hope's triumphant
   laurel
Entwined its wreath about the widow's moral ;
Her sky of promise spanned an ocean's shore
Too vast for boundless fancy to explore ;
And when her thought, exultant, sought to be
Personified in its vastidity—
When whispering voices told her of the fame
Which splendor lent to grace a widow's name,
She vowed, that let whoever might importune,
Henceforth she'd live the mistress of her fortune !
Her heart and hand, thank God, were free again ;
The former felt no lingering trace of pain !
A pious pilgrimage, made once a year
   To the joint tomb which held a sacred trust,
Enabled her to drop a sorrowing tear,
   Upon the sod of its comingling dust.
She sought the place in Autumn's solemn time,
When Nature's sadness had a voice sublime ;
And though the birds and latest flowers had
   flown,

She dashed the grave with perfume of cologne.

A stately port and beautiful complexion,
  The widow boasted still, at thirty-eight;
But there were some who said, on close inspec-
    tion,
  (Perhaps from envy, or what's worse, from
    hate.)
That rouge assisted nature; and the toilet
Which gave the tint, if left unmade, would
    spoil it.
It mattered little whether this were so;
Her stately figure had a healthful glow;
Her rounded arm for sculpture might have been
A perfect model, to adorn a queen,
Or "shape the subject of a painter's dream."
Aglaia-like, she boasted all the graces,
And carried off the palm from pretty faces.
Her acquirements bore an inverse ratio
  To her pretensions. Several works of fiction

By standard authors; such as Swift, Boccacio,
   Cervantes, Scott, (she chose them for their
     diction,)
Were her familiars. She could also play
   The piano, which is indispensable
In one whose aspirations point the way
   To leadership in fashion's ranks ostensible.
But she was wise, as serpents are, and knew
A power like theirs, to charm a certain few,
Her coterie contained within its ranks,
Two or three prizes, and a score of blanks.
The latter bowed subservient to her will;
Her smile created, and her frown could kill;
What she applauded, left no other choice;
For theirs was but the echo of *her* voice;
What she condemned, was doubly damned at
     sight,
If censure gave her mood the least delight.
Thus her dominion was the rule of might.

Exalted beauty claims exalted state,
   Where wealth administers with lavish hand;
And though the widow's learning was not great,
   She had that certain prestige of command
Which overawes the plebeian of letters,
Who bows to rank, but smirks upon his betters.
She moved among the fashionable throng,
Like one to whom superior rights belong,
And seemed to win, not ask the homage ren-
   dered,
As something due where it was humbly ten-
   dered.
Where pleasure reigned, to dissipate the hours,
Pre-eminently shone her gifted powers;
Her rustling silks had music in their tone;
Her diamonds with a double lustre shone;
The roses in her hair contrasted finely
With curls which hung about her neck divinely.
Her ivory shoulder shone above its prison
Of lace and velvet, like a moon, new-risen;

And where her bodice ceased to offer cover,
The spectacle was one to craze a lover;
(This custom finds its hosts of imitators,
And never fails to *draw* on woman-haters!)

   Since she denied herself another union,
The widow found her heart sighed for commu-
   nion;
Her friends, nor pleasure's constant round, could
   render
That happiness she hoped to find in splendor.
A lover of convenience would not do,
For that was wicked, and brought scandal, too;
A parrot she already had, whose screaming
At night, awoke her from her pleasant dreaming;
The madrigals her mocking-bird discoursed her,
Of late from all the joys of home divorced her.
·She would not, as prescribed, procure a monkey;
That character shone out in every flunky
Who loitered in her parlors; till she hated

Their subjects, and the tones in which they
    prated.
What would she do ? The season is advancing
When gaiety holds revel—routs and dancing—
The glorious waltz, ecarte, whist, tableaux,
In forms of splendor to her vision rose !

Oh, blest invention ! Woman' fertile mind
    Explores thy vast arcana with success ;
    And bears a trophy from thy dark recess !
Which slumbering ages failed to know or find!
A single idea, brilliant and inspiring
Sprang into birth when hope lay half expiring !
A brain like her's was rapid in expedient ;
It grasped results, regardless of ingredient ;
Device and subterfuge, though near of kin,
Take different courses on the road to sin ;
The one discovers what the other chooses,
And here analogy its office loses.
The widow, then, had found a grand device,

Untainted with the least degree of vice ;
And thus it flashed into the light of day—
HER DOORS SHOULD OPEN TO A PROTEGE !
She seldom paused to note, or calculate
The horoscope impending o'er her fate,
But yielded gracefully to what befel ;
She therefore reached, and touched a silver bell.
"Paper and pen and ink," she proudly said ;
A servant heard, and instantly obeyed.
"Now, village beauty," thus she mused, while
    holding
A letter written, and prepared for folding ;
"Though Hebe's gifts and Thisbe's love-spell
    bound thee,
I'll cast the toils of city life around thee ! "
So said, and so dispatched, the letter sought
Its destination; freighted with the thought
But partly uttered, though completely writ,
In the next chapter, where we follow it.

PART II.

Never did muse experience great desire
To snatch from heaven the true Promethean
    fire,
And pour its flame into her similies,
So much as mine ; which grasps at all she sees,
To warm and spur the lagging pace of these.
Replete with obstacles, her eye surveys
A trodden field, containing faded bays ;
Where genius, gleaning in the days gone by,
Took every thought of earth, and air, and sky ;
Leaving the modern author like a stem,
Stripped of the rose, which was its diadem.

Let us suppose a picture.   Such an one
  As life presents at many a fire-side ;
The out door labor of the day is done ;
  The ledger balanced—credit and debit side ;
A family group, assembled round the hearth
  As evening closed, with cold and sombre shade,
Alternate gave its smile, to cheer the mirth
  Which half-a-dozen romping children made ;
At nine o'clock, the latter went to bed,
After the usual nightly prayer was said.
A venerable man presided here ;
All that his failing years held high or dear,
Were clustered round him.   In his stout old
    heart
He wore them as its green and better part.
His wife and daughter sat beside him still,
  Plying the needle, smiling and conversing ;
Care had no voice, nor time a void to fill ;
  Simple and brief their stories.   The rehears-
    ing
       *

Becomes not history. They were satisfied ;
Their bliss was unassuming in its pride.
The knocker strikes ! A mutual glance and
   flutter
   Betray surprise.   It was some neighbor visi-
   tor ?
The grocer, or the dairyman, with butter ?
   Some gossip-vender, or perhaps, inquisitor
After the village paper? which, to borrow,
With promise to " return again to-morrow,"
Has been a custom since the days of Faust,
With those who seek to read at others' cost.
It could not be a burglar ; in your village,
Such gentry rarely attempt rapine or pillage.

Who was it knocked ?   The reader may in-
   quire ;
   And properly enough.   But first in place,
The younger lady's name is called Elvira,
Who responded to the signal with a grace,

And opened the door.   The postman's visage
    met her ;
He made his bow, and handed her a letter.

A letter by post !   That was indeed a rarity !
    In towns remotely situated, stages,
Like " angels' visits," or a deed of charity,
    Are semi-occasional.   Something else engages
The quiet minds of people who possess
Within themselves the means of happiness.
The locomotive, and the rattling car ;
Rumors of purchase, and impending war ;
Convulsive throbs in business speculations ;
Exploding banks and stock-job operations ;
Might form a globe, and have a common axis
The same to them, so they escaped the taxes.
But to the letter !   Elvira broke the seal.
It was addressed to her—an eloquent appeal,
Or rather, pressing invitation proffered,
To " come and share the home a cottage offered,

Where music dwelt, if beauty but awoke it,
To joyousness, such as the past bespoke it."
A waxen signet, elegantly done,
Was underwritten—LUCY HARRISON.
The second postscript, out of some half-dozen,
Appealing to the father, as her cousin,
Denied his right, from any fond compunction,
To interdict the force of her injunction.
The fourth and fifth, contained much special
    pleading,
To prove Elvira needed " city breeding,"
With interlarded expletives on morals,
Which graced the theme, like ornamental corals.

It would have pleased a physiognomist
    To note the marked effect the letter had;
The old man being a philanthropist,
    His countenance was rarely ever sad.
It was a question to his thinking, best
Decided on the instant.   His request

Was a decree, so qualified and just
That hearing was to recognise and trust.
He blessed Elvira, telling her to go;
" She was his cherub, and he wished it so."
The mother wept; but did not interpose
Objections. Elvira's happiness arose
Above all selfish feeling; and she said,
" Her husband's word was law, to be obeyed."

  Elvira was young, and full of wild romance;
It flushed her cheek, and sparkled in her glance;
She longed for action—novelty—the stirring
Events, which make up city life—occurring
To interest and occupy the hours
Of pleasure's votaries; with odorous flowers
And fragrant blossoms in ideal vases,
Such as imagination's pencil traces.
Her father's love, a bountiful reliance,
Made the request, and called for her compliance.

PART III.

It is a stupid kind of situation,
This sleepy pace of family narration;
Casting the characters in proper order;
To one the post of ward, another warder;
Of heroine and hero, as expected,
If authors' stories are to be respected.
At once, then, let the thing be understood,
    Elvira took two days for preparation;
Called on her friends about the neighborhood,
    Telling them she should visit a relation.
(How near of kin, her father had not stated,
Although she knew they *really* were related,)

Received the compliment of many kisses
From doating mamas and pathetic misses.
Some tears were shed ; so basely crocadile
That they provoked, in spite of her, a smile.

One other scene remained of interview.
     Elvira loved.   Could maiden youth survive
That halcyon period, when the skies are blue—
     The flowers fragrant, and a busy hive
Of glowing thoughts is struggling in the breast
Of ardent natures—giving them unrest—
 . And keep their honey sacred ?   Books declare,
     And countless teachings of the old traditions,
That selfishness may flourish everywhere,
     With barbarous tribes, and in the Christian
          missions ;
Among the Esquimaux, and Barolongs, and
          savages
     On Frazer River, or the Rocky Mountains ;
Leading to warfare, and all kinds of ravages

Suggested by the malice of its fountains—
Excepting only in a woman's soul,
When it first bows to love's sublime control.
Her's was a shrine erected to Justinian,
    A village magnate, and a noble youth;
Who filed his claim to the supreme dominion
    Of its devotion, and its virgin truth.

PART IV.

If curious people—some are always curious
To ascertain the current from the spurious—
Had tarried, on the 20th of December,
(A date I hope the reader will remember,)
To note a throng of busy dealers—they might
Have caught a gleam of gossip's radiant day-
    light.
These dealers carried hampers, fowls, confec-
    tions,
Cakes, boxes, jars, and fruits of all complex-
    ions;

Guavas, lemons, sugars, cordials, spices,
Besides a quantity of wines and ices;
With many other delicacies, savored
To suit the palates of the highly favored.
And set them down, each parcel, one by one,
Before the door of Mrs. Harrison.
Her cottage mansion was a kind of palace—
A target for the envious shots of malice—
With inner glories, such as poverty
Had no conception dwelt with luxury.

The widow's purpose was a *fete*—Elvira
    At any moment might drop in upon her.
A journey of two hundred miles, would tire a
    Much stronger constitution; it had done her
So, many times; in fact, whene'er she made it,
She had experience, therefore, when she said it.

Elvira came—a coming duly bruited,
    And was thrice welcomed by a host of friends;

Even before her strength had been recruited.
The smile of fashion its approval lends
To such occasions, where the obligation
Is felt to be a courtesy of station;
These were the widow's friends, and her's by
    parity
Of reasoning.   The forms of etiquette
Admit, constructively, of such familiarty.
    Breeding's a thing that no one should forget;
It is not based upon those cold punctilios
Ascribed to upstarts and the supercilious;
But gushes forth from genial hearts spontaneous,
As now, in kind entirely miscellaneous.
The widow met her handsome ward, enfolding
    Her healthful form within a warm embrace;
A tribute of affection worth beholding
    Especially when practiced with a grace.
The other ladies understood their cue,
And welcomed her with their embraces too!

Elvira stood uncovered. The widow's eyes
Were fixed upon her in a blank surprise.
"My darling child! How could they so de-
  ceive me!
  They said you were a handsome hoyden
    grown;
And now, by all that's beautiful, believe me,
  A fairer brow on woman never shown!
That blush, too! Stay thy blushes; let me
  speak,
And kiss again, the ruby on that cheek!
What eyes; what lips; what teeth, and hands,
  and stature;
(I will be heard in mine own nomenclature.)
What motion! Dearest, thou art wholly mine;
We'll teach all meaner beauties how to shine!"
(The closing words, that others might not hear,
Were whispered softly in Elvira's ear.)

The Cyclops and Briareus, in a Pantheon

Of demi-gods, such as professor Tooke
Has furnished schools, to whet the classic
    fancy on,
With their achievements noted in his book,
Were very opposite in the kind of function
Which each received with heaven's especial unc-
    tion;
Briareus had a hundred heads, and hands
Some fifty, to enforce his dread commands;
Besides a savage courage, truly Roman
    Or Grecian—(both those ancient nations knew
    him;)
The monster felt secure, and cared for no man,
    Till Jupiter caught hold of him, and threw him,
Bound fast in chains, under the mountain Etna,
Not quite so pleasant as a trip to Gretna!

The Cyclops—(how capricious Fortune varies
    Her favors!   Even in a luscious mouth,
Whose breath should be like perfumes from the
    South,

She introduces the detested caries!
Pugs up a nose, casts in the eye strabismus,
Or plays some other naughty prank to quiz us!)
The Cyclops had a single eye—" a buster,"
As modern phrase would style it; full of luster,
Directly on the frontal bone located:
And this was what discriminating Fate did.

" Well, where's the application?" do you ask?
   Indeed, that 's rather difficult to tell;
The muse has ventured on a thankless task,
   (I only hope she may discharge it well,)
And means to say, perhaps, that Mrs. Harrison
Outdid Elvira, when in the comparison
Of talkers—one discharged a ceaseless battery
Of words amounting to the sheerest flattery;
At least the other thought so. While she lis-
   tened,
A tear-drop on her drooping lashes glistened.
It might have been, to know that she possessed

B

Sufficient charms to make a woman blest ;
But, judging from her innocence and youth ;
Her soul as spotless as the shrine of truth,
It were, no doubt, a very wise conclusion,
To say her tears resulted from confusion.

It has been shown how prodigally lavish
  The widow was of money, to prepare
A *fete* of royal splendor, that should ravish
  All rival hearts, and fill them with despair.
It was her right, conforming to her humor;
She gloried in the wide-extended rumor
Which spread abroad among the fashionable,
Of viands purchased to adorn her table ;
Of music—some said fully fifty pieces—
Of crimson furbelows and lacy fleeces ;
Candelabrum of gold, and those rich oddities
Which Turks and Chinese deal in as commod-
      ities ;
Including flowers, indiginous and exotic,
In such profusion as to be chaotic.

None who knew her doubted her ability
To entertain with lady-like nobility.

Had my muse the florid, terse felicity
Of Butler's pen, aside from all complicity
With plagiarism; this story Hudibrastic,
Constructed of a language wholly plastic,
Descriptive, liquid, metrical and pungent,
Should flash with wit and metaphor abundant.

It is too late to falter. Onward! then;
Let criticism do its spite ; and when
The public condemnation—or what's even worse,
Silent contempt, bestows its mildew curse
Upon her efforts ; " let it be understood "—
As valiant Artaximines declared—
"She would have done much better, if she could,"
And of their praises, not their censure, shared.

PART V.

Wise heads regard it as a curious riddle,
   Without solution, (which is still more curious,)
That the tortuous cat-gut of a fiddle,
   However softly touched—however furious—
In daytime fails completely to inspire
   Those exquisite emotions of the night,
Which waken in the soul a soft desire
   Beneath a flood of artificial light.
Per contra: It is equally mysterious,
   That febrile constitutions cannot bear
The sun's departure; they become delirious
   From simply breathing night's mephitic air;

And how revolting are the teas and physic
To invalids, confined with croup or tisic!

Our grandads and grandames, who were "old
    fogies,"
Accoutered in their homespuns and their "sto-
    gies,"
Before the age of hacks and patent leather,
   Thought nothing of a journey of five miles,
Despite the threatening signs of "wind and
    weather,"
   Across the fields, surmounting "stubs and
    stiles,"
To join the "break down" of a Highland fling,
Or solus, cut a graceful "pigeon-wing!"
Like "Cousin Sally Dilliard," if a brook
Should intervene upon the route they took,
They did not stop to grumble or beshrew it,
But tucked their dresses up and waded thro' it!
Their custom was, to "start" the dance at seven,
And keep it going "constant" till eleven.

Apropos of such an hour.   The twenty-first
Of December, like a meteor, burst
Upon the world of fashion.   From its dawning,
The moments had been occupied in conning,
Furbishing and stitching.   The mantua-makers
Perfumers, hair-dressers and undertakers
Of toilet duty, reapt a silver crop
Of dimes and dollars.   Mrs. Fitzlollypop
For two whole nights and crucifying days,
Kept herself tightly laced in patent stays,
Under instructions from a fancy milliner,
And had a vertigo, which came nigh killing her.

The Thompson sisters met with a disaster
    Not quite so serious, but decidedly more
      stupid ;
They used upon their cheeks a kind of plaster,
    Or poultice, termed " The Fairy Charm of
      Cupid,"
To whiten the complexion, and to soften
The skin, as they had done with success often.

This beautifier, in the general fidget
Which prevailed, being mixed by Irish Bridget
With acids instead of Lubin, scarified
And burnt the spot to which it was applied.

Eleven had struck, P. M.; and then a rumbling
   Of carriages broke on the listening ear;
At first it seem'd like distant thunder, grumbling;
   But this was not the season of the year
For thunder. There were a hundred, less or
   more,
All of which drove directly to the door
Of Mrs. Harrison's house, or rather gate,
And there discharged their valuable freight.

The age is given to progression; therefore,
It is not every why that has its wherefore;
Our penurious grandads and grandmamas,
If they preferred their homespuns and ban-
   danas,

And early hours, and primitive seclusion
To costly equipage and gay profusion,
That was their matter—a bliss of ignorance
Containing neither merit, wit nor romance.

If the antipodes were joined, not parted
By intervening space; if hollow-hearted
People were anomalies; if anything
Which is impossible, through time should wing
Its flight to earth; if even happy Lazarus
In Abraham's bosom sought to gather us;
We would pronounce the exploit a miracle,
And exercise the right to doubt it still.
On this hypothesis, it would be idle
To strip Pegassus of his croup and bridle.

Let us look into those magnificent rooms,
All redolent of splendor and perfumes;
Not to attempt description; they defied it;
As any one might find, who vainly tried it.

The charming widow and her ward were standing
Within the center of the room, commanding
A general view. As the gay company entered,
Of course, all eyes upon the twain were centered.
An usher named the guests, who first paid duty
Unto the hostess ; next, to the blushing beauty,
Who in due form received a presentation
As "a loved friend and visiting relation."

Oh, human heart ! how varied thy emotions !
    With depth and surface; where alternate hope
And fear predominate—like a vast ocean's
    Calms, and billows ; love's sweet kaleidoscope,
Giving to thoughts disjointed and erratic
A symmetry and coloring prismatic—
In thy divinest workings there is fault;
The fetid odors of a charnel-vault
Contain no matter equally putrescent
With thy malice, surmounted by the crescent
Of hate and envy—above all other sins
Begotten of Satan's dam—unsightly twins.

Many a *coiffure*, set off with sprigs and roses,
   (To cover locks of silver-sprinkled hair,)
Many a bosom, where the cross reposes,
   (As if the crucifix possessed a virtue there!)
Concealed what alchymists, with all their science,
Could not fathom—a voiceless, proud defiance
Against Elvira; who, poor innocent, had not
The least conception of their envious thought.

The obverse side of bosoms and of heads,
   Like medals, graven to perpetuate
A deed of history; their meaning sheds
   To magnify the praises of the great;
And to be read aright, must be turned over
As printed pages are, within a cover.
Had she not beauty of a kind resplendent,
Niether on art nor artifice dependent?

Miss Littlejohn, who joined the promenade
   Hanging upon the arm of her admirer,

A scrutiny and criticism made
Of everything pertaining to Elvira.
" She certainly is pretty ; so is glass
When stained, or marble, with a final polish ;
But I could count a dozen as they pass—
For instance, Mrs. Myrtle, or Miss Dollish,"
Quoth she, " as evidently her superior,
As these fine gildings to the room's exterior !
How shabbily she dresses ! and how gawkish !
Even the dimensions of her *robe battante*
Are circumscribed to a degree that's mawkish !
Perhaps the stuff was rather dear and scant ?
And in the village where the girl was taught,
Such articles are at the grocer's bought !"

PART VI.

It is not only fortunate that we
Cannot "see in ourselves what others see,"
Or our defects, of pyramidal size,
Would shut us from the hopes of Paradise;
As orbs pursuing their assigned ellipse,
Obscure the sun with shadows of eclipse.
Of equal wisdom is that Providence
Which teaches there's atonement for offence;
So that our virtues, in the general reckoning,
Toward the goal of happiness keep beckoning;
Holding us in the path of rectitude,
" Whose ways are pleasantness," and truly good.

Elvira noted nothing. A conflicting
　　Tumult of passions moved upon her soul,
Which her weak powers failed of interdicting.
　　Her nature was not of those that can control
The current of events, when it is flowing
Directly in the course she would be going.
The music, like a dream, warm and impassioned,
　　With ideal shapes each flitting object fashioned;
And twenty mirrors, flashing back the light
Of gold and diamonds on her ravished sight,
Seemed life, and spring, and happiness supernal,
Whose gushing rhapsodies would prove eternal.

She yielded wholly to the spell. It bore her
　　As zephyrs bear the blossoms; floating, glanc-
　　　　ing
In air and gaslight; everything before her
　　Partook of bliss and beauty; and the dancing—
(Especially as practiced now-a-days;
An arm completely round a lady's stays;

B*

The cheeks in contact, with a sudden whirl,
Enough to dizz and startle any girl—)
Confused her senses; as it truly might,
In one who never witnessed such a sight,
Nor, mingling in its mazes, felt the charm
Of being clasped by man's supporting arm!

Is not the world a heaven at such a time,
When bounding hearts in guilelessness sublime,
Untrammeled by the mercenary fears
Which desecrate their shrine in after years,
Exalt, in their own exaltation, merit
Conceived or real, without wish to blur it!
Who has not felt it?　Let him know the death
Which hopeless felons die; no sacred breath
Of prayer or priestly consolation given,
For such a soul deserves to die unshriven!

'Tis said affliction has a common level
　For prince and peasant; high and low degree;

The case is different where the sound of revel
  Predominates ; rank shuns affinity
With meaner objects ; and all meaner ties
Than fashion's pomp, its votaries despise.

Captain Bombuster, in his epaulettes,
A very trifling circumstance forgets,
To wit : that his income by commutation,
Largess and salary, fall below his station.
If his indulgent creditors pushed the matter,
(Inclusive of tailor, bootmaker and hatter,)
The reveille which "beat him up to quarters,"
Would shock his nerves much more than shells
  or mortars.

Professor Hartshorn, with the curved proboscis,
Lately composed a famous diagnosis
On the diseases of poodles ; see him strut,
Like Gulliver, a giant in Lilliput.
For half a million, generally confessed
His realty and personal stand assessed,

He was also the inventor and patentee
Of an incomparable pill ; and he
Arose from nothing, (how very funny !)
By the sheer force of impudence and money.

Behold Miss Perripool, and mark the history
Which properly becomes a part of this story.
Her crimson satin and her diamond set,
Who sees will not be likely to forget.
She is a banker's daughter.   Every fold
Of her black hair is intertwined with gold ;
Pearls, amethists, carbuncles, sapphires mingle
In unison of blaze ; her flounces jingle
With bugles and tassels, elaborately wrought ;
   Found only in the bazaars of foreign traders,
And all the way from the East Indies brought,
   To ornament her person.   The invaders
Of African deserts and sacred antiquities
Had rifled their stores, the lady's taste to please.
This peerless beauty boasted that her dress
Cost full ten thousand—not a penny less.

A year ago her sire, the banker, failed
   For something like a million—maybe more ;
Who could depict the misery entailed ?
   Not even the ocean, in its angry roar,
Sends up to heaven complainingly, a moan
So terribly appalling, as the groan
Of the poor orphans, widows and mechanics,
(Who always suffer most by business panics,)
To find themselves within a tyrant power,
Which crushed their life out in a single hour.

The banker survived, as bankers always do ;
Three months elapsed, and he commenced anew ;
Communities get into quite a fever
   At such events ; and so, to keep them still,
The lawyers call for some one as *Receiver*—
   A kind of modern financial miracle,
Generally chosen from the legal ranks,
As having greater knowledge of the banks.

He takes the assets and holds them; (holding
    means,
In the vocabulary of these go-betweens,
Using—a sort of term convertible,
When the assets are gold and silver—portable!)

The banker survived. Why not? His credit
    Was good as ever. He had sympathisers;
And he was honest! Every person said it;
    Except the envious, and the heartless misers.
The "Receiver" had compromised his liabilities
At five cents on the dollar. Let hostilities
Be buried. It was a shame that rancor
Should seek to persecute an honest banker!

There stands a lady, portly and majestic;
    Her necklace first-water diamonds, to the tune
Of three thousand dollars. Her domestic
    Affairs are in a state of healthful bloom;
Her sideboards groan beneath the massive weight
Of Bohemian glass-wares and of costly plate;

Chargers of silver ; tea-sets of the same ;
Carpets from Turkey ; vases of porcelain ;
A stately mansion on a prominent street ;
Form but the merest epitome of her complete
Establishment. Fashion's seal indorses
Her diploma ; its vignette a span of horses
Attached to a splendid carriage, with outrider
In livery. Mark you the man beside her !
It is her husband—one who wears the sandal
Shoon of that denomination. Scandal
Says very many wicked things ; in his case
They have been proven execrably base.
And so in hers. However cold and haughty
Her manner seems to him, 'tis only thought a
Shrewd invention, to mislead those prying mon-
    gers,
Whose appetite for gossip always hungers.

This gentleman—a merchant—Mr. Emery,
From earliest youth. possessed a treacherous
    memory,

And one day signed, unwittingly, a paper
Drawn on the foreign house of Pugg & Draper,
For eighty thousand dollars; which came back
Protested; but alas! and oh, alack!
It found him penniless; his stock of good assigned
To whom, or why, the sheriff could not find.
(It cannot be amiss just here to menton,
None doubted honest Emery's intention
To do the fair thing.   Yet, somehow or other,
The draft—a forged one—got him into pother!)
He was convicted, sentenced—but his friends
Obtained a pardon.   Here his story ends.
That of his wife "hath this extent, no more,"
She was a nameless seamstress; one who bore
An excellent character, above suspicion.
She married Emery, and her changed condition
Is here apparent—free of all hypocrisy;
And they are patterns for our aristocracy!

There sits a plain and common kind of person,
  At least, so far as dress denotes the man;

Some Smith, or Jones, or Johnson, or McPherson,
   Completely under ostracism's ban.
His being there, no doubt was condescension,
The reason why, the hostess failed to mention.
Scarcely a glance of favor falls upon him ;
It was the cue to overlook and shun him.
His shabbiness is painful. He lacks caste.
He is the stubble of a harvest past !
He might have been a Satrap, or Bashaw,
   A Grand Mogul, or even Haroun Alraschid ;
'Twas wrong to freeze, when such a general
   thaw
Prevailed there. Why not do as the mass did
Assume a part ? Almighty Jupiter Tonans,
   Magnus Apollo, or irresistible Narcissus,
Born of the Turks, the Persians, or Greeks, or
   Romans,
   Would lose identity among these dames and
   misses,
If modesty controlled them, and they chose
To visit such a place in shabby clothes.

He was, in fact, a gentleman and scholar,
Who worshipped science, and despised the dollar;
His graceful pen was known to all the leaders
　　In literary circles—but to these people,
Critics in gossip's idle world, not readers—
　　His achievements might tower like a steeple—
A forest of chaplets cluster round his name,
Smith or McPherson suited them the same.
He was deficient in the ornamental;
A thing to them important and essential.

Fond Mrs. Harrison stood by Elvira,
　　Or rather, followed her with watchful glances,
Hers was a form could readily inspire a
　　Feeling of joy in woman. It enhances
Their self-love at the half-way house of life
(In one who has discharged the cares of wife,)
To recognise some feature in these elves,
Reminding them of what they were themselves.
She counseled as a mother might ; (that is
A fashionable mother ;) taught her how to quiz

The gentlemen, and draw them kindly to her,
Either to serve her purpose, or to woo her.
(Few women require instructions on such points,
   They have a mother wit to supercede it,
Which man's philosophy so utterly disjoints
   That he's a fool who will not pause and heed it.)

So passed the fleeting time, till the fair daughters
   Of Sol and Chronis waked their drowsy sire ;
His rising beams flashed o'er a world of waters,
   And robed the sky in tints of liquid fire.
The revellers disbanded, in the haze
Of early morning.   Byron aptly says—
" Ladies who have been dancing, or partaking
   Of any other kind of exercise,
Should make their preparations for forsaking
   The ball-room ere the sun begins to rise,
Because, when once the lamps and candles fail,
His blushes make them look a little pale !"

PART VII.

The muse indulges one of "fancy's freaks,"
   And finds the license come in proper play,
To bring the reader forward some six weeks,
   For which indulgence she "will ever pray,
And so forth," as they sign it in petitions
For certain objects, "subject to conditions."

Elvira corresponded with Justinian
   And others of her friends, some three or four;
And in her letters gave a free opinion
   Of what she heard and saw. See if it bore
Resemblance to itself, in all the changes
Through which imagination sometimes ranges:

"Dearest," (to Justinian, letter number one,)
"That naughty woman, Mrs. Harrison,
Has kept my brain so constantly excited,
Perplexed, amazed, and dizzy and delighted,
That l am hardly fit to write a letter,
Even to you, who know me so' much better
Than others ; and would a fault excuse,
When they might harshly censure, and refuse.
Last night she gave a *fete*, by far more gorgeous
Than those of tho Capulets, or regal Borgias,
At Verona and Ferara ; (you remember,
We saw them at the play, in all their splendor :)
And Justinian, darling ! would you guess,
This *fete* was given to *me !*   "It would impress,"
So Mrs. Harrison said, " upon the gay
A proper respect for her young protege."
I don't admire the ladies much.   They stare
One wholly out of countenance ; and repair
To separate corners of the room, in *squads,*
(A military term ; but where's the odds?)

C·

Accepting only such polite attentions
As come from gentlemen of high pretensions.
I thought, at first, there was a lack of breeding
In such a very singular proceeding.
But Mrs. Harrison said not; which made me
Feel rather cheap, and afterwards "keep shady."

Nothing of this kind had the least effect
On my behavior ; though I half suspect
That Mrs. Harrison whispered it, *sub rosa ;*
(It was no harm, Justinian, to suppose a
Case like this!) *I was a youthful heiress!"*
If that was wrong, may Heaven in pity spare us!

I hear you ask me, "Did you make a conquest ?'
What then?   Think you such secrets are con-
    fessed ?
Mr. Bodu, be sure, a clever fellow,
Whom the champagne had made a little mellow;

Protested much, and put his arms around me,
('Twas in the waltz,) as if he would confound me.
There was a tremulous fervor in his speech,
Eloquently fluent—much beyond the reach
Of my weak intellect; and his dark eye
Could penetrate into the soul! But why
Write thus to you, my dear Justinian? Fear not,
My heart is thine, and thou art not forgot!"

Elvira was ingenuous; (but art
In woman's nature plays a leading part;
She may not feel it, think it, or design it,
Much less have skill to fathom or define it;
Consummate, prompt, effective, often wise,
It is the spell in which her power lies.)
She loved Justinian; such a love as " grows
On what it feeds;" to doubt her, or suppose
That it was not devoted and impassioned,
Was to mistake her nature, which was fashioned
For such a sentiment. She lacked the wit
To act a part, or play the counterfeit.

The sky of pleasure has a brilliant glow;
Its tide is onward in a peaceful flow.
Elvira, guided by the skillful hand
Of Mrs. Harrison, ventured out from land
Upon its seething waters.   Each excess
Of sweet indulgence brought new happiness.
The shade of Scylla, and Charybdis' roar,
If seen or heard, were far towards the shore.
Theaters, entertainments, operas, balls,
Country excursions, pic-nics, morning calls,
Were daily pastimes—nightly continuities
In fashion's train of elegant congruities.

It is a period of just four weeks
Since Elvira's arrival; her glowing cheeks
Are moist with tears.   Why weeps the maiden?
Is her young heart with sorrow overladen?
She takes a pen; the quietude invites;
Her pride is up, and this is what she writes:
"Justinian, you're in error.   Mr. Bodu

Would not have said such cruel things of you.
When in a better humor, write.   Adieu."

The golden links of that romantic chain
   Which early love had linked, are loosed and
   broken ;
Never to fetter those two souls again,
   Nor hang about them as a mutual token.
Absence and doubt—sisters in evil doing—
Completely intercept the work of wooing.

The final letter : " Justinian, let the past
   Be all forgotten.   I can bear the shock.
We are too young to have a shadow cast
   Upon the future.   Jealousy's a rock
Which shatters the affections.   Your suspicions
   Have done me great injustice ; but no matter ;
I neither ask nor offer you conditions !
   My language must not be construed to flatter
A hope of other thought or other feeling
Than that which now is spoken.   The concealing

Might do us both dishonor in the end.
Farewell, Justinian.   Deem me still thy friend!"

Mrs. Harrison read the letter over,
   (Her cunning had suggested it) and said
" *That* was the way to cure an upstart lover,
   Obscurely born, and purely country-bred!"

" Nothing is true but Heaven;" nothing sure
Excepting sorrow and death; and nothing pure
But Truth's eternal principle, which bears
A golden fruit, amid surrounding tares!

Two years have passed.   The handsome protege
Is an acknowledged leader in the gay
And fashionable circles; she has caught
The inspiration of the thing ; and brought
Her accomplishments to such perfection,
That she no longer " musters for inspection."
The widow's purse, containing any amount—
Aye, even the freedom of her bank account,

Bestows its shining tribute to support
A grandeur worthy of Eugenie's court.

"Can such things truly be, and not excite
    Our special wonder?"   Did Roman Crœsus
(As rich as he was valiant in a fight)
    Compose an essay, or devise a thesis,
Explanatory of the great disparity
Existing between a bounty and a charity?

One frosty morning, about the hour of ten,
    A gentleman inquired for Mrs. Harrison;
It was her lawyer—one of the shrewdest men
    That in the lists of legal talent shone.
After the usual ceremonies, he
    Proceeded to enlarge upon his business.
What has he said!   The widow trembles; see
    How pale she grows! She faints from sudden
    dizziness!

He told her plainly, that her real estate,
. Which yielded her such princely revenues,
For some time being mortgaged, with the date
    Of a foreclosure pending, she must choose
To let them go for nothing, or redeem them.
    He had done all he could for a renewal,
And truth will out ! (an artist should have seen
        them !)
    Hoping she would not think his mission cruel—
The titles were defective and disputed !
Soon as the question had been fairly mooted,
He gave the deeds a thorough overhauling,
And found the fact apparent as appaling !

" This is not all.   Madam, do me the favor,"
    Said he, " to cast your eye upon this note ;
It came directly from your money-shaver,
    Who seems to study your affairs by rote.
He says your credit has been overdrawn,
And he must have your jewelry in pawn."

A ship thrown on it beam-ends by typhoon;
A sudden darkness spread across the moon;
A hail-storm in mid-summer; the infecting
   Breath of contagion, poisoning the air,
When happy homes and hearts are least sus-
   pecting
   Such visitation—may produce despair;
But not that paralyzing sense of horror
Which struck the widow speechless in her sorrow.
Her bark was foundered. Life's phantasmagoria,
Once luminous with dancing figures, bore a
Forbidding aspect. That stately pride of hers
Was humbled amid her servile worshippers.

Elvira must not know the full extent
Of this calamity. What tale would she invent
To perpetrate a subterfuge, and close
The drama in dramatic style? She chose
The following: Mr. Bodu believed
Elvira an heiress. He was no more deceived

In that, than she in him. *His* treachery
Was half conceived in love, and all in lechery.
That gentleman—a pink of the *beau monde*,
The widow addressed by missive, " to respond
At once, without excuses ; something serious
Suggested to her language thus imperious !"
Bodu obeyed—obeying was his forte
When paper missives "summoned him to court."

" Sir," said the lady, (they are snugly closeted,)
    " Our friendship has been mutual ; but built
Upon a sandy basis, if deposited
    To screen a fault, or palliate a guilt.
We have had secrets, too ; and may have, yet ;
If your devotion, like a parapet,
Is capable of shielding what it loves—
If feeling blended with affection, moves
Your noble heart, as generous as 'tis large,
To throw its ægis round a double charge.
Briefly, Bodu—as time will not delay,
You must espouse Elvira, and to day !

I am a bankrupt! Read the Sheriff's warning
To quit these premises to-morrow morning!"

"Power is godlike!" (Richelieu's apothegm.)
  Possessed by mitred priest or Roderick Dhu;
It is the monarch's peerless diadem,
  Prerogative—command; the sword which slew
Dentatus, with his back against the rock,
When fifty foes assailed him with its shock.
It is the mere inditing of a word,
To bind the captive, or unloose the herd;
The despot's safeguard, and the tyrant's knell;
Begotten in heaven, but usurped in hell!

A smile, contemptuous, pitiless, sardonic,
  Gleamed like a shadow over Bodu's face,
While his reply, implacably laconic,
  Revealed a heart unutterably base.
" Madam!" (the prologue had an ominous sound,
Which struck the shaft still deeper in its wound,)

"Madam,' said he, "the day is. past when
    duty
Exerts itself to meet the claims of beauty;
I fear your plans have very much miscarried;
It cannot be—*I am already married!*
This is *my* secret.   See that it is kept!"
He sought the door, and o'er its threshold leapt :
The widow groaned despairingly, and wept.

Our days, like tide-rifts, on a troubled stream
    Have different currents, whose collisions mark
A darkened line, with effervescing sheen,
    Threatening destruction to a heedless bark.
But even in the depths of those dark tides
A fascination irresistible abides.
The fearless diver, to their caves descending,
Heeds not the peril with his passion blending,
Which caution's finger often designates,
But cannot avert : " The coward hesitates,"
Is the belief of some men, but an error;
Caution alone controls and masters terror.

This was the fatal theory on which
Misguided Lucy Harrison, once rich
To the excess of magnificence, stumbled,
And from the loftiest height of fashion tumbled.

Whether we will or not, Time flies apace,
  Defying human effort to o'ertake him ;
Ambition's utmost reach lags in the race
  To circumvent, or catch, or hold, or make him
Correct anachronisms in his diary :
He is too fleet a courser, and too fiery.
We can but follow his eventful track,
And note the days and hours by looking back.

So, let us indulge a retrospect.   Twelve years
  Have intervened since that lugubrious day
Which left the widow Harrison in tears.
  It is the season of Spring—the first of May;
When forests and fields assume their garniture,
When hopes are brightest, and the wind with
    pure

And fragrant breath, stirs gently in the leaves,
And noisy swallows twitter on the eves ;
The scene lies in a village.   There's a rout
Among the children—school has just let out ;
And they are curbed from childish glee and prank
To join a marching column—two in rank,
For pic-nic purposes.   The noted feature
Of this occurrence, is a female teacher ;
A spinster lady, proud and grave in action,
Who does not feel that perfect satisfaction
Which such a spectacle, at such a time
A certain class of people think sublime.
Emotions very foreign to equanimity
Are felt by minds awakened to sublimity.
She took by the hand, and led, a blooming lad,
    Another's offspring, but a favorite child ;
Her countenance was inexpressibly sad,
    When she looked down upon him—loosing its
        mild
And placid expression—a kind of despair
Or melancholy seemed to settle there.

Doubtless her heart contained some recollection
Sacred and secret from the world's inspection.
She kissed the boy, a double kiss, and said—
"Justinian, go and mingle in the sports;"
Not feeling just as she felt, he obeyed.
 And here our closing history reports
What might be very easily comprehended
Without the writing—long ago had ended
Elvira's dream of love, and her career
Of fashion's folly; acted in a sphere
Above her means and village education;
And yet, beneath that dignity of station
Which gentlemen and ladies thorough-bred
Wear as a vestal virtue, to be shed
Like sunlight, or perfume, broadcast around
 them,
Seeking to cheer the lowly— not to wound them.

There is a level for all men and things,
  Which liquids very aptly illustrate;
And whether below, or soaring high on wings,
  We seek to avoid the inevitable fate;
The sequel has an arbitrary spot,
Where it indites a eulogy or blot!